Praise for
THE WHITE BOOK

"Formally daring, emotionally devastating and deeply
political . . . In this subtle and searching novel, Han,
through Smith, proposes a model of genuine empathy,
one that insists on the power of shared experience but
is not predicated on the erasure of difference."
—KATIE KITAMURA,
The New York Times

"*The White Book* is a novel that's difficult to describe, but
easy to love. It's a delicate book, hard to know, impossible to pin down, but it's filled with some of Han's best
writing to date. . . . And it's also one of the smartest
reflections on what it means to remember those we've
lost."
—NPR

"A brilliant psychogeography of grief, moving as it does between place, history and memory . . . [The prose is] poised and never flinches from serene dignity. . . . A mysterious text, perhaps in part a secular prayer book . . . Translated peerlessly by Smith, [it] succeeds in reflecting Han's urgent desire to transcend pain with language."

—*The Guardian*

"With eloquence and grace, Han breathes life into loss and fills the emptiness with this new work."

—*Library Journal*

"Everything I ever thought about the color white has been profoundly altered by reading Han Kang's brilliant exploration of its meaning and the ways in which white shapes her world, from birth to death—including the death of *The White Book*'s narrator's older sister, who died just a few hours after she was born, in her mother's arms. This is an unforgettable meditation on grief and memory, resilience and acceptance, all offered up in Han's luminous, intimate prose."

—*Nylon*

"Han's first two English-language translations . . . were instant sensations, establishing her as a riveting practitioner of the surreal and of historical fiction alike. Her latest . . . is told by a woman haunted by the death of her elder sister just after birth—a contemplation of life, death, resilience and, as the title hints, color."

—*HuffPost*

"An astonishingly rendered work of fiction . . . precise, subversive, fierce and deceptively opaque . . . In its own way the novel is a sublime expression of grief's incongruous byways, its busy inactivity, its larger, more elaborate intrusions."

—*Financial Times*

"[*The White Book*] promises to be equal parts Italo Calvino, Angela Carter, and something entirely Han Kang's own. . . . A quieter, yet just as intensely symbolic, follow-up to the startling violence of her first two books."

—*LitHub*

"Intensely personal, hypnotically serene, and mournfully meditative."

—*Asian Review of Books*

THE WHITE BOOK

흰

THE WHITE BOOK

HAN KANG

Translated from the Korean by Deborah Smith

HOGARTH

London / New York

Published in the United States by Hogarth, an imprint of
Random House, a division of Penguin Random House LLC, New York.

HOGARTH is a trademark of the Random House Group Limited, and the
H colophon is a trademark of Penguin Random House LLC.

Originally published in Korean as 흰 by Munhak Dongne,
Seoul, in 2016. This translation originally published in Great Britain
by Portobello Books, London, in 2017. This edition published by
arrangement with Portobello Books.

ISBN 978-0-525-57307-4
Ebook ISBN 978-0-525-57308-1

Printed in the United States of America on acid-free paper

randomhousebooks.com

9 8 7 6 5 4 3 2 1

Book design by Lauren Dong

1

I

나

In the spring, when I decided to write about white things, the first thing I did was make a list.

Swaddling bands
Newborn gown
Salt
Snow
Ice
Moon
Rice
Waves
Yulan
White bird
"Laughing whitely"
Blank paper
White dog
White hair
Shroud

With each item I wrote down, a ripple of agitation
ran through me. I felt that yes, I needed to write
this book and that the process of writing it would be
transformative, would itself transform into something
like white ointment applied to a swelling, like gauze laid
over a wound. Something I needed.

But then, a few days later, running my eyes over
that list again, I wondered what meaning might lie in
this task, in peering into the heart of these words.

If I sift those words through myself, sentences will
shiver out, like the strange, sad shriek the bow draws
from a metal string. Could I let myself hide between
these sentences, veiled with white gauze?

This was difficult to answer, so I left the list as
it was and put off anything more. I came abroad in
August, to this country I'd never visited before, got
a short-term lease on an apartment in its capital, and
learned to draw out my days in these strange environs.
One night almost two months later, when the season's
chill was just beginning to bite, a migraine set in,
viciously familiar. I washed down some pills with warm
water and realized (quite calmly) that hiding would be
impossible.

*

Now and then, the passage of time seems acutely apparent. Physical pain always sharpens the awareness. The migraines that began when I was twelve or thirteen swoop down without warning, bringing with them agonizing stomach cramps that stop daily life in its tracks. Even the smallest task is left suspended as I concentrate on simply enduring the pain, sensing time's discrete drops as razor-sharp gemstones, grazing my fingertips. One deep breath drawn in and this new moment of life takes shape as distinctly as a bead of blood. Even once I have stepped back into the flow, one day melding seamlessly into another, that sensation remains ever there in that spot, waiting, breath held.

Each moment is a leap forward from the brink of an invisible cliff, where time's keen edges are constantly renewed. We lift our foot from the solid ground of all our life lived thus far and take that perilous step out into the empty air. Not because we can claim any particular courage, but because there is no other way. Now, in this moment, I feel that vertiginous thrill course through me. As I step recklessly into time I have not yet lived, into this book I have not yet written.

Door

This was something that happened a long time ago.

Before signing the contract for the lease, I went to look
at the apartment again.

Its metal door had once been white, but that
brightness had faded over time. It was a mess when
I saw it, paint flaking off in patches to reveal the
rust beneath. And if that had been all, I would have
remembered it as nothing more than a scruffy old door.
But there was also the way its number, 301, had been
inscribed.

Someone—perhaps another in a long line
of temporary occupants—had used some sharp
implement, maybe a drill bit, to scratch the number
into the door's surface. I could make out each
individual stroke: 3, itself three hand spans high; 0,
smaller, yet gone over several times, a fierce scrawl that
attracted attention. Finally, 1, a long, deep-gouged line,
taut with the effort of its making. Along this collection

of straight and curved wounds rust had spread,
a vestige of violence, like long-dried bloodstains,
hardened, reddish-black. *I hold nothing dear. Not the place
where I live, not the door I pass through every day, not even,
damn it, my life.* Those numbers were glaring at me,
clenching their teeth shut tight.

That was the apartment I wanted that winter, the
apartment where I'd chosen to spin out my days.

As soon as I'd unpacked, I bought a can of white paint
and a good-size paintbrush. Neither the kitchen nor
the bedroom had been repapered, and their walls
were spotted with stains large and small. These dark
splotches were especially conspicuous around any
electrical switches. I wore pale gray tracksuit pants
and an old white sweater, so the splatters wouldn't
show up too badly. Even before I'd started to paint,
I was unconcerned with achieving a neat, even finish.
It would be enough, I reasoned, just to paint over the
stains—*surely white splotches are better than dirty ones?* I
swept my brush over the large patches on the ceiling
where the rain must have seeped through at one time,
watching gray disappear beneath white. I gave the
sink's grubby bowl a wipe with a washcloth before

painting it that same bright white, never mind that its pedestal was brown.

Finally, I stepped out into the corridor to paint the front door. With each swish of the brush over the scar-laced surface, its imperfections were erased. Those deep-gouged numbers disappeared, those rusted bloodstains vanished. I went back inside the apartment to take a break and get warm, and when I came back out an hour later I saw that the paint had run. It looked untidy, probably because I was using a brush rather than a roller. After painting an extra coat over the top so the streaks were less visible, I went back inside to wait. Another hour went by before I shuffled out in my slippers. Snow had begun to scatter down. Outside, the alley had darkened; the streetlights were not yet on. Paint can in one hand, brush in the other, I stood unmoving, a dumb witness to the snowflakes' slow descent, like hundreds of feathers feathering down.

Swaddling bands

Swaddling bands white as snow are wound around the newborn baby. The womb will have been such a snug fit, so the nurse binds the body tight, to mitigate the shock of its abrupt projection into limitlessness.

Person who begins only now to breathe, a first filling-up of the lungs. Person who does not know who they are, where they are, what has just begun. The most helpless of all young animals, more defenseless even than a newborn chick.

The woman, pale from blood loss, looks at the crying child. Flustered, she takes its swaddled self into her arms. Person to whom the cure of this crying is as yet unknown. Who has been, until mere moments ago, in the throes of such astonishing agony. Unexpectedly, the child quiets itself. It will be because of some smell. Or that the two are still connected. Two black unseeing eyes are turned toward the woman's face—drawn in the direction of her voice. Not knowing what has been set in motion, these two are still connected. In a silence shot through with the smell of blood. When what lies between two bodies is the white of swaddling bands.

Newborn gown

My mother's first child died, I was told, less than two hours into life.

I was told that she was a girl, with a face as white as a crescent-moon rice cake. Though she was very small, two months premature, her features were clearly defined. I can never forget, my mother told me, the moment she opened her two black eyes and turned them toward my face.

At the time, my parents were living in an isolated house, in the countryside near the elementary school where my father taught. My mother's due date was still far off, so she was completely unprepared when, one morning, her water broke. There was no one around. The village's sole telephone was in a tiny shop by the bus stop—twenty minutes away. My father wouldn't be back from work for another six hours.

It was early winter, the first frost of the year. My twenty-two-year-old mother crawled into the kitchen and boiled some water to sterilize a pair of scissors.

Fumbling in her sewing box, she found some white cloth that would do for a newborn's gown. Gripped by contractions and terribly afraid, she plied her needle as tears started down. She finished the tiny gown, found a thin quilt to use as swaddling bands, and gritted her teeth as the pain returned, quicker and more intense each time.

Eventually, she gave birth. Still alone, she cut the umbilical cord. She dressed the bloodied little body in the gown she'd just made, and held the whimpering scrap in her arms. For God's sake don't die, she muttered in a thin voice, over and over like a mantra. After an hour had passed, the baby's tight-sealed eyelids abruptly unseamed. As my mother's eyes met those of her child, her lips twitched again. For God's sake don't die. Around an hour later, the baby was dead. They lay there on the kitchen floor, my mother on her side with the dead baby clutched to her chest, feeling the cold gradually enter into the flesh, sinking through to the bone. No more crying.

Moon-shaped rice cake

Last spring, someone asked me whether I'd had
"a particular experience, when you were young, which
brought you close to sadness." For a radio interview.

Faced with that question, it was this death that
came to me. It was a story that I had grown up hearing.
The most helpless of all young animals. Pretty little
baby, white as a moon-shaped rice cake. How I'd been
born and raised in the place of that death.

"White as a moon-shaped rice cake" never made
much sense until, at six, I was old enough to help
out with making the rice cakes for Chuseok, forming
the dough into small crescent moons. Before being
steamed, these bright white shapes of rice dough are
a thing so lovely they do not seem of this world. Only
afterward, dished up on a plate with a pine-needle
garnish, did they become disappointingly matter-of-
fact. Glistening with roasted sesame oil, their color
and texture transformed by heat and steam, they

were tasty, of course, but utterly unlike that former loveliness.

So when my mother said "white as a rice cake," I realized, she meant a rice cake before it is steamed. A face as startlingly pristine as that. These thoughts made my chest grow tight, as though compressed with an iron weight.

Last spring, in the recording studio, I didn't mention any of this. Instead, I spoke of my pet dog, which died when I was five years old. He was an unusually intelligent dog, I said, a mongrel, but descended in part from the famous Jindo breed. I still have a black-and-white photo of the two of us, a candid shot of an intimate moment, but, strangely enough, I cannot remember him alive. My one vivid memory is of the morning when he died. White fur, black eyes, still-damp nose. From then on I developed an aversion to dogs that has persisted to this day. Rather than reaching out to tousle soft fur, my arm stays clamped to my side.

Fog

Why do old memories constantly drift to the surface
here in this unfamiliar city?

When I go out into the streets, the scraps of
conversation that pull into focus when the speaker
brushes past me, the words stamped on street and
shop signs, are almost all incomprehensible. At times
my body feels like a prison, a solid, shifting island
threading through the crowd. A sealed chamber
carrying all the memories of the life I have lived and
the mother tongue from which they are inseparable.
The more stubborn the isolation, the more vivid these
unlooked-for fragments, the more oppressive their
weight. So that it seems the place I flee to is not so
much a city on the other side of the world as further
into my own interior.

The early hours of the morning, and the city is cloaked
in fog.

The border between sky and earth has been

scrubbed out. The only view my window offers is the blurred suggestion of two poplars, ink-wash contours wavering four or five meters up from where the street lies hidden; all else is white. But can we really call it white? That vast, soundless undulation between this world and the next, each cold water molecule formed of drenched black darkness.

I remember a morning on an island long ago, when the fog had been as thick as this. A walk along a cliff path with the others in the group. Pine trees flickering in and out of existence. Towering ashen cliff. The backs of my companions' heads, which seemed eerily blank and hard-edged as they peered down at the black waters shifting beneath the thick sea fog. But how ordinary a scene that same path showed when I walked it again the following afternoon. What I had fancied a mysterious swamp was a dry, dust-clogged puddle. The pine trees, which had seemed otherworldly when seen in snatched glimpses, were cordoned off by a stretch of barbed wire. The sea's deep blue had the sheen of a tourist postcard. Everything was back within its own borders, holding its breath. Holding its breath and waiting for the next fog.

What do the ghosts of this city do, these muffled early-morning hours?

Slip soundlessly out to walk through the fog that has been holding its breath and waiting?

Do they greet each other through the gaps between those water molecules that bleach their voices white? In some mother tongue of their own, another whose meaning eludes me? Or do they only shake or nod their heads, without the need for words?

White city

I saw some footage of this city, taken by a US military aircraft in the spring of 1945. The film was screened in the projection room on the first floor of the memorial hall, situated in the east of the city. The subtitles said that over a period of six months, starting in October 1944, 95 percent of the city was obliterated. This city, whose people rose up against the Nazis, from which the German soldiers were driven out in September 1944 and where a month of civilian government was achieved, hence Hitler's decision to use any means necessary to sweep it clean out of existence as an example.

When the film opened, the city seen from far above appeared as though mantled with snow. A gray-white sheet of snow or ice on which a light dusting of soot had settled, sullying it with dappled stains. The plane reduced its altitude, and the city's visage sharpened. There was no snow covering it, no soot-streaked ice. The buildings had been smashed to pieces, literally pulverized. Above the white glow of stone ruins were blackened flecks as far as the eye could see, showing where the fire had touched.

Riding the bus back to my apartment, I got off at the park, which I'd heard housed a very old castle. After a while walking through its forested grounds, I came upon an old hospital building. A faithful reconstruction of a building that had been destroyed in a 1944 air raid, no longer used as a hospital but as an art gallery. As I passed along the narrow trail, vaulted with a mass of intertwined tree limbs, where the birds' high trill put me in mind of skylarks, it occurred to me that all of these things had at one time been dead. These trees and birds, paths and streets, houses and trams, and all of these people.

In this city there is nothing that has existed for more than seventy years. The fortresses of the old quarter, the splendid palace, the lakeside villa on the outskirts where royalty once summered—all are fakes. They are new things, painstakingly reconstructed based on photographs, pictures, maps. Where a pillar or perhaps the lower part of a wall happens to have survived, it has been incorporated into the new structure. The boundaries that separate old from new, the seams bearing witness to destruction, lie conspicuously exposed.

It was on that day, as I walked through the park, that she first came into my mind.

A person who had met the same fate as that city. Who had at one time died or been destroyed. Who had painstakingly rebuilt themselves on a foundation of fire-scoured ruins. Who was therefore something new. Who, some broken pediment having survived, has ended up bearing a strange pattern, the new distinct from the old.

Certain objects in the darkness

Certain objects appear white in the darkness.

When darkness is imbued with even the faintest light, even things that would not otherwise be white glow with a hazy pallor.

At night, I make up the sofa bed in the corner of the living room and lie down in that wan light. Instead of trying to sleep, I wait, feel my senses attune to the passage of time. The trees outside the window cast silhouettes onto the white plaster wall. I think about the person who resembles this city, pondering the cast of their face. Waiting for its contours to coalesce, to be able to read the expression it holds.

The direction of the light

I read an account by a man born in this city, in which
he claimed to have lived for as long as he could
remember with the soul of his elder brother, who had
died at the age of six in the Jewish ghetto. The child's
voice came to him from time to time, he said, with
neither form nor texture. In addition, the language
was foreign to him, as he'd been adopted by a Belgian
couple and grown up in that country, meaning he
hadn't at first been able to tell that the speaker was
his brother. It could only be a waking dream, he
thought, in which everything is doomed to recur, or
else a symptom of derangement. When, at the age of
eighteen, he finally came to learn of his family history,
he began to study the language of this country, to
understand what this soul was trying to tell him. And
thus he learned of his brother's fear, this brother both
older and younger. That he was screaming the same
terror-struck words, choked out when the soldiers had
come to arrest him.

*

I slept badly for several days after reading this, unable
to stop my thoughts from turning to the final moments
of that six-year-old child, who would ultimately have
been murdered. In the small hours of one such restless
night, when the roiling inside me had finally calmed,
it occurred to me that if I had been similarly visited
myself, by my mother's first child who had lived just
two hours, I would have been utterly oblivious. Because
the girl had never learned language at all. For an hour
she had held her eyes open, held them in the direction
of our mother's face, but her optic nerves never had
time to awaken and so that face had remained beyond
reach. For her, there would have been only a voice.
Don't die. For God's sake don't die. Unintelligible words,
the only words she was ever to hear.

And so I can neither confirm nor deny that there are
times when she has sought me out, hovering at my
forehead or by the corners of my eyes. That some
vague sensation I had known as a child, some stirring of
seemingly unprompted emotion, might, unbeknownst
to me, have been coming from her. For there are
moments, lying in the darkened room, when the chill

in the air is a palpable presence. *Don't die. For God's sake don't die.* Turned toward indecipherable sounds laden with love and anguish. Toward a pale blur and body heat. Perhaps I, too, have opened my eyes in the darkness, as she did, and gazed out.

Breast milk

The twenty-two-year-old woman lies alone in the
house. Saturday morning, with the first frost still
clinging to the grass, her twenty-five-year-old husband
goes up the mountain with a spade to bury the baby
who was born yesterday. The woman's puffy eyes will
not open properly. The various hinges of her body
ache, swollen knuckles smart. And then, for the first
time, she feels warmth flood into her chest. She sits up,
clumsily squeezes her breast. First a watery, yellowish
trickle, then smooth white milk.

She

I think of her living to drink that milk.

I think of stubborn breathing, of tiny lips mumbling at the nipple.

I think of her being weaned and then raised on rice porridge, growing up, becoming a woman, making it through every crisis.

I think of death deflected every time, faced with her back as she moves firmly forward.

Don't die. For God's sake don't die.

Because of those words knitted into her, an amulet in her body.

And I think of her coming here instead of me.

To this curiously familiar city, whose death and life resemble her own.

Candle

As I have imagined her, she walks this city's streets.
At a crossroads, she sees a section of redbrick wall. In
the process of reconstructing yet another shattered
building, the wall had been taken down and rebuilt a
meter in front of its original position, along with a low
epitaph explaining that the German army used it to line
up civilians and shoot them. Someone has put a vase
of flowers in front of it, and several white candles are
crowned with wavering flames.

Wreaths of fog still shroud the city, less thick than
in the early morning, translucent as tracing paper.
If a strong wind got up and skimmed off the fog,
the ruins of seventy years ago might be startled into
revealing themselves, pushing out from behind the
present reconstructions. The ghosts that were
gathered there, very close to her, might stand up
straight against the wall where they were slaughtered,
their eyes blazing out.

But there is no wind, and nothing is revealed

beyond the already apparent. The warm white candle wax creeps ever downward. Feeding themselves to the white wicks' flames, these stubs sink steadily lower, eventually out of existence.

Now I will give you white things,

What is white, though may yet be sullied;
Only white things will I give.

No longer will I question

Whether I should give this life to you.

2

—

SHE

그
녀

Rime

The window is not quite flush in its frame, allowing rime to form on its glass. Midwinter. That pattern of frozen white recalled the snow ice that forms on a stream's surface. The writer Park T'ae-won said that just such a window had drawn his gaze when his first daughter was born, hence the name he coined for her: Seol-yeong. Snow flower.

She'd once seen the sea itself frozen over. An unusually shallow stretch of water, compounded by a cold current, had formed serried ranks of frozen waves, like layer upon layer of dazzling white flowers captured in the moment of unfurling. She saw frozen fish strewn over the sandy shore, the hard glint of their scales. On such days, the people of that region say "the sea is rimed over."

Frost

The day she was born was one of frost rather than
snow, yet her father chose *seol,* snow, as one of the
characters for his daughter's name. Growing up,
she was unusually sensitive to the cold and resented
the chill embedded in her name.

    But she liked to tread the frost-covered ground
and feel the semifrozen earth through the soles of her
sneakers. The first frost, as yet untrodden, has the
fine crystals of pure salt. The sun's rays pale slightly
as the frost begins to form. White clouds of breath
bloom from warm mouths. Trees shiver off their leaves,
incrementally lightening their burden. Solid objects
like stones or buildings appear subtly more dense.
Seen from behind, men and women bundled up in
heavy coats are saturated with a mute presentiment,
that of people beginning to endure.

Wings

It was on the outskirts of this city that she saw the
butterfly. A single white butterfly, wings folded on a
reed bed, one November morning. No butterflies had
been seen since summer; where could this one have
been hiding? The air temperature had plummeted
in the previous week, and it was perhaps on account
of its wings frequently freezing that the white color
had leached from them, leaving certain parts close
to transparent. So clear, they shimmer with the black
earth's reflection. Only a little time is needed now and
the whiteness will leave those wings completely. They
will become something other, no longer wings, and the
butterfly will be something that is no longer butterfly.

Fist

Walking this city's streets until her calves had grown
stiff, she waited. For something of her native language,
sentences or even mere scraps of words, to surge
swiftly to the tip of her tongue. She thought she might
be able to write about snow. In this city, where they say
it snows for half the year.

She kept a dogged watch for the coming of winter.
Studied the shop windows, the reflections shown there
not yet blurred by streaks of snow. The heads of others
passing through the streets, still with no powdery
dusting. Those slanting forms, not yet snowflakes,
barely grazing the foreheads of strangers. Her own
cold fists, which she clenched to white.

Snow

Against the background of a black coat sleeve, a large
flake of snow will reveal its crystals even to the naked
eye. A scant couple of seconds and she has witnessed
it all. Mysterious hexagons melting clean away.

When it first begins to fall, people stop what they
are doing and turn their attention to the snow. On
a bus, they lift their eyes from their laps and gaze out
of the window for a time. Once the snow has been
soundlessly strewn about, with an equal absence
of joy or sorrow, and the street's erasure is complete,
the people turn their faces away, and the blurring
streaks are no longer reflected in their eyes.

Snowflakes

One late night long ago, she'd seen a man lying at
the foot of a telegraph pole. He was slumped on his
side. Had he fallen? Was he drunk? Should she call
an ambulance? While she vacillated, unable to move
away from the scene yet wary of drawing nearer, the
man heaved himself halfway up and focused his blank
gaze on her. She flinched, startled; though there
seemed no immediate threat of violence, the alley was
otherwise deserted. She walked on with hurried steps,
then turned to look back. The man was squatting on
the cold pavement, still in the same awkward position,
staring piercingly at the grimy white wall that stretched
along the alley's opposite side.

> he who had shipwrecked himself in an alley,
>> who had pushed himself up on cold-numbed
>> hands,
> thinking of what his life has been,
> of the loneliness that waits for him at home,

thinking what is this, what the hell is this
damned dirty white

falling snow.

Sparse flakes fly in all directions.
In the black air where the streetlights do not
    touch.
Whirled above the black branches of wordless
    trees.
Brushing against the bowed heads trudging
    through the night.

Perpetual snow

She'd considered living somewhere in sight of
perpetual snow. Where the bodies of trees clustered
close outside her window would mark each shift in
season against the unchanging backdrop, off in the
distance, of permanently ice-capped mountains. Cool
as the hands on her fevered forehead when she lay at
home on a school day.

There was a black-and-white film made here in
1980, in which the protagonist lost his father when he
was seven years old and was raised by his calm, gentle
mother. (His father had been only twenty-nine when
he met with disaster, climbing the Himalayas with a
group of friends. His body was never found.) The son
moved out of his mother's house as soon as he was
old enough, and lived by an incredibly strict code of
ethics. Whenever he had to make a decision, he would
see in his mind's eye an oppressive landscape: fresh
snow falling on the icebound Himalayas, like a whiteout
inside his head. Each time, he made the choice that

went hardest with himself, the choice that many others would have quailed at. In a period when corruption was rife, he alone refused to take bribes and for that he was ostracized, even physically attacked. In the end, he walked into a trap, was hounded out of his place of work, and returned home alone. There, allowing himself to become lost in thought, the peaks and ravines of that far mountain range filled up his field of vision. The very place where he could not go. The land of ice, in which his father's frozen body was hidden, where humans were not suffered to tread.

Wave

In the distance, the surface of the water bulges upward.
The winter sea mounts its approach, surging closer
in. The wave reaches its greatest possible height and
shatters in a spray of white. The shattered water slides
back over the sandy shore.

Standing at this border where land and water meet,
watching the seemingly endless recurrence of the
waves (though this eternity is in fact illusion: the earth
will one day vanish, everything will one day vanish),
the fact that our lives are no more than brief instants is
felt with unequivocal clarity.

Each wave becomes dazzlingly white at the moment
of its shattering. Farther out, the tranquil body of water
flashes like the scales of innumerable fish. The glittering
of multitudes is there. The shifting, stirring, tossing of
multitudes. Nothing is eternal.

Sleet

There is none of us whom life regards with any
partiality. Sleet falls as she walks these streets, holding
this knowledge inside her. Sleet that leaves cheeks and
eyebrows heavy with moisture. Everything passes.
She bears this remembrance—the knowledge that
everything she has clung to will fall away from her and
vanish—through the streets where the sleet is falling,
that is neither rain nor snow, neither ice nor water, that
dampens her eyebrows and streams from her forehead
whether she stands still or hurries on, closes her eyes
or opens them.

White dog

What's a dog that's a dog but doesn't bark?

She was a child when she first heard this riddle. When, or from whom, she doesn't remember now.

The summer when she was twenty-four, when she'd quit her first job and gone back to the house she'd grown up in, she saw a white dog in the neighbors' yard. Previously, this had been the home of a vicious Tosa, originally bred as a fighting dog. It used to rush forward, stretching the rope as taut as it would go, and snap its jaws. All it needed was for the rope around its neck to be loosened or to snap for it to fly at you and sink its teeth into your flesh. Though she knew the dog was tied up, she still kept as far away from it as possible whenever she had to pass the gate, intimidated by its viciousness.

Chained up now in that Tosa's place was a mongrel with perhaps a faint strain of Jindo blood. Its body was dotted with patches of bare flesh, pale pink coins amid the dull white of its fur. This dog neither barked nor even growled. When it first met her eye, it drew back, startled, the chain around its neck rasping over the cement floor. It was August, and the scorching sun was unrelenting. Perhaps because of the muggy heat, the road through the village was deserted. The silence was broken only by the chain's harsh grating each time the dog flinched back. At her slightest movement it startled afresh, pressed itself even farther to the floor, and scrabbled back, dragging the chain over the cement. Keeping its eyes fixed on her the whole time. Terror. It was terror that she read in those two black eyes.

That evening she asked about the dog. "It doesn't even bark if it sees a stranger," her mother said, "just cowers and trembles, so the owner's thinking of selling it on again. What if a burglar came?"

The dog never lost its fear of her. Even on her last day at home, when it had had a full week to become used to her, it cringed close to the ground and jerked backward as soon as she appeared outside the gate. It twisted its head against its flank as though something was pressing against its windpipe. Though its tongue lolled out between its teeth, there was no audible panting. The only sound the dog could be said to produce was the low rasp of the chain against the cement. Even the sight of her mother, a familiar face of several months' acquaintance, would provoke this same startled reaction. *Okay, now, it's okay.* Her voice was soft and soothing as she walked unhurriedly on. *Poor wretch,* she muttered, clicking her tongue, *it must have suffered a lot.*

A dog that's a dog but doesn't bark?

The lackluster answer to the riddle is fog.

And so for her, the dog's name became Fog. A large white dog that doesn't bark. A dog that bore a physical resemblance to her childhood pet, now a hazy memory from the distant past.

That winter when she went down again to her family home, there was no Fog. Instead, she was greeted by a squat brown bulldog that snarled with great gusto.

What happened to that other dog?

Her mother shook her head.

The owner had it for sale the whole summer, but he couldn't quite bring himself to part from it; then when the frost came and the temperature suddenly dropped, it died. It got sick and stopped touching its food, just lay there on its front . . . and the whole time, it didn't make a single sound.

Blizzard

A few years ago there was a heavy-snow warning.
Seoul was in the grip of a blizzard as she walked alone
on a hill path. Her umbrella proved next to useless at
keeping the snow off. She carried on walking, white
flakes whirling thick and fast around her face and
body. Unable to fathom what on earth it could be, this
thing so cold, so hostile. This vanishing fragility, this
oppressive weight of beauty.

Ashes

That winter, she and her younger brother made a six-
hour drive to a beach on the south coast. The box
holding their mother's powdered bones they enshrined
in an ossuary; the small temple nearby with a view of
the distant sea would house the woman's soul. The
monks would chant her name with their sutras in the
early hours of each morning. On Buddha's birthday a
paper lantern would be lit in her memory.

With those voices, those lights near at hand, our
mother's ashes would lie in changeless calm inside a
sealed stone drawer.

Salt

One day she took a handful of coarse salt and
examined it closely. Those crystals had a cool beauty,
their white touched with gray. For the first time,
she had a real sense of the power that lay within this
material: the power to preserve, the power to sterilize
and to heal.

There had been a time before that when she was
preparing food and picked up salt with an injured hand.
If letting the knife slip was the first mistake, made
because she was pressed for time, allowing salt to touch
the unbandaged cut was the second, and the worst.
That was when she'd learned how it actually felt, the
expression "to pour salt in the wound."

Some time later, she saw a photograph of an
installation in which a hill of salt had been constructed,
on which visitors were then invited to rest their bare
feet. After sitting in the chair that had been put there
for that purpose and removing your shoes and socks,
you put both feet up on the salt and could sit like that

for as long as you wanted. The photograph showed a dark exhibition space, with the only spot of trembling light being the summit of the salt hill, which was a little taller than the height of a person. The exhibition visitor, whose face was in shadow, sat in the chair with her bare feet resting on the slope of salt. Perhaps because she had been like that for a long time, the white salt hill and the woman's body appeared to have fused together, naturally and painfully.

To do that, she thought, studying the photograph, *you'd have to have feet with no wounds or scars. Only if my feet were fully healed could I rest them on that mountain of salt. Where the shade retains a certain chill, however white it shines.*

Moon

When clouds swim in front of the moon and obscure
its light completely, those same clouds instantly shine
white and cold. When black clouds are mixed in with
the white, a delicate chiaroscuro is formed. Behind that
pattern of dappling dark, the wan moon is concealed,
wreathed with ashen or lilac or pale blue light, full or
halved or a shape more slender still, waning to a single
sliver.

Each time she gazed up at the mid-month moon,
she would see a person's face. Ever since she was very
young, all the grown-ups' explanations had fallen on
deaf ears: she never could manage to make out the
shapes she was told were there, the pair of rabbits and
the mortar they pound rice in. All that was apparent
were two eyes, seemingly lost in thought, above the
shadowed suggestion of a nose.

On nights when the moon is unusually large, she
can leave the curtains open and let its light flood

every inch of her apartment. She can pace then, up and down. In the light filtering out of a huge white pondering face, the darkness soaking out of two black eyes.

Lace curtain

Is it because of some billowing whiteness within us,
unsullied, inviolate, that our encounters with objects
so pristine never fail to leave us moved? Her passage
through the frozen streets brings her to the building,
where her gaze lifts to the second floor. To the flimsy
lace curtain hanging there.

There are times when the crisp white of freshly
laundered bed linen can seem to speak. When that
pure cotton fabric grazes her bare flesh, just there, it
seems to tell her something. You are a noble person.
Your sleep is clean, and the fact of your living is
nothing to be ashamed of. Such is the strange comfort
she receives, at that in-between time when sleep
borders wakefulness, when that crisp cotton bedsheet
brushes her skin.

Breath cloud

On cold mornings, that first white cloud of escaping
breath is proof that we are living. Proof of our bodies'
warmth. Cold air rushes into dark lungs, soaks up the
heat of our body, and is exhaled as perceptible form,
white flecked with gray. Our lives' miraculous diffusion,
out into the empty air.

White birds

A congregation of white gulls on the winter shore. Around twenty, perhaps? The birds were sitting facing out to sea, where the sun was creeping down to the horizon. As though observing some kind of silent ceremony, holding themselves perfectly still in the subzero cold as they witnessed the day's decline. She stopped walking and let her gaze follow theirs, to that pallid source of light that was about to flush crimson. Though the cold was so severe it seemed to sink its teeth right down to her bones, it was precisely the heat from that light, she knew, that kept her body from freezing.

A crane by the water's edge, one Seoul summer's day. Entirely white save for its bright-red feet. The bird was picking its way out of the water and up onto a smooth, broad rock. Was it aware of her gaze? Perhaps. And also that she meant it no harm? Hence its impassive expression as it faced the opposite bank, letting the sun's rays dry its red feet.

Why do white birds move her in a way that other birds do not? She doesn't know. Why do they seem so especially graceful, at times almost sacred? Now and then, she dreams of a white bird flying away. In the dream, the white bird is very close, so close it seems she could reach out and grasp it as it flies forward, beating its wings in utter silence, the sunlight slanting off its feathers. It flies far away, and yet, somehow, never beyond the reach of her gaze. Gliding through the air, eternally unvanishing. Its dazzling wings fanned out from its sides.

What should she make of it, the white bird alighting briefly on her head and then flying off again, here in this city? She'd been on her way home, fretting about something, trudging through the park and along the stream's bank. Something swooped down and settled its huge self on the crown of her head. After extending both wings so that they enveloped the sides of her face like a wimple, the tips of its feathers almost brushing her cheeks, it lifted away and flew to the roof of a nearby building, as though it had had no business with her at all.

Handkerchief

She saw it one afternoon in late summer, as she was
walking past a secluded tenement building. A woman
on the second floor was hanging her washing out over
the balcony rail when a handful of items slipped from
her grasp. A single handkerchief drifted down, slowest
of all, finally to the ground. Like a bird with its wings
half furled. Like a soul tentatively sounding out a place
it might alight.

Milky Way

Once winter set in, almost every day in this city was overcast, and she could no longer see the stars in the night sky. The air temperature dropped below zero, and a pattern began in which days of continuous rain alternated with days of snow. The low air pressure gave her frequent headaches. The birds hugged the ground as they flew. The sun began to set at around three o'clock in the afternoon, and by four it was utterly dark.

As she walked, raising her eyes to the afternoon sky a black that her homeland knew only at night, her mind turned to thoughts of nebulae. To the thousands of stars like grains of salt whose light had streamed down to her, those nights at her parents' countryside home. Clean, cold light that had bathed her eyes, scouring her mind of all memory.

Laughing whitely

The expression "laughing whitely" (probably) exists only in her mother tongue. Laughter that is faint, cheerless, its cleanness easily shattered. And the face that forms it.

"You laughed whitely, you know."
    In this instance, "you" would (probably) be someone who managed to force a laugh, quietly enduring some internal struggle.

"He laughed whitely."
    Here, "he" would (probably) be someone struggling to part from something inside himself.

Yulan

Two of her university classmates died in relatively swift succession, one at the age of twenty-four and one at twenty-three. The former in a bus crash, the latter during his military service. A few months after this second accident, in early spring, former students from the same graduating class got together to purchase two yulan saplings, which they planted on the hill on the university grounds, overlooking the classroom where the two students had studied literature together.

Some years later, walking beneath those flowing trees, which spoke of life—rejuvenation, revivification—she wondered: What made us choose yulan? Because white flowers have to do with life? Or with death? She'd read somewhere that the words "blank" and "*blanc*," "black," and even "flame," literally "fire flower" in Korean, all have the same root in Indo-European languages. Blank white flowers of fire, blazing in the surrounding dark—the brief March blooming of two yulans.

Small white pills

Now and then she finds herself wondering, and not out of self-pity, but with a detached, almost idle curiosity: If you could add up all the pills she'd ever taken, what would the total be? How many hours of pain has she lived through? As though life itself wished to impede her progress, she was brought up short again and again. As though the force that prevents her moving forward to the light stands always at the ready inside her own body. All those hours when she had lost her way, in hesitation and in doubt. How many would there be? How many small white pills?

Sugar cubes

She was around ten years old at the time. Her first outing to a coffee shop, accompanied by her aunt, was also the first time she set eyes on sugar cubes. Those squares wrapped in white paper possessed an almost unerring perfection, surely too perfect for her. She peeled the paper carefully off and brushed a finger over that granular surface. She crumbled a corner, touched it to her tongue, nibbled at that dizzying sweetness, then eventually placed it in a cup of water and sighed as she watched it melt away.

She isn't really partial to sweet things anymore, but the sight of a dish of wrapped sugar cubes still evokes the sense of witnessing something precious. There are certain memories that remain inviolate to the ravages of time. And to those of suffering. It is not true that everything is colored by time and suffering. It is not true that they bring everything to ruin.

Lights

In this city of severe winters, a December night
unspools itself around her. The darkness outside
the window has no moon to soften it. In the small
workshop to the rear of the building, presumably as
a security measure, a dozen electric lights are left
on all through the night. She looks at the patches of
illumination, scattered and isolated amid the black.
Since she came to this place, or no, in fact before, her
sleep has been scattered and shallow. Even if she did
drop off for a while, she would rise to find the world
just as dark as before. If, by some stroke of luck, she
were able to manage a longer sleep, the blue tinge of a
sluggish dawn would be seeping steadily from within
the black. Yet those lights will be frozen white as ever,
in the clarity of their stillness, in their isolation.

A thousand points of silver

On such a night, without the slightest reason, the sea surges up.

The boat is so small that even the slightest wave sends it pitching and yawing violently. Eight years old and afraid, she crouches in the bottom of the boat, shoulders hunched. At just such a moment, a thousand points of silver sweep in from the distant sea and pass beneath the hull. In an instant she forgets her fear, gazing wide-eyed after the turbulent motion of that glittering immensity.

An anchovy shoal, her uncle says laughing. He had been sitting in the stern the whole time, barely batting an eyelid. A tangled mop of curly hair above a swarthy face. He never did see forty: his addiction to alcohol would carry him away in the space of two years.

Glittering

What is it about minerals that glimmer, like silver, gold, or diamonds, that makes people think of them as noble? One theory puts it down to the fact that, for early man, the glittering of water signaled life. Shining water meant clean water. Only water that is drinkable—that gives life—is transparent. Whenever, after trekking through deserts, forests, and fetid swamps, a group was able to discern a body of water glittering white in the distance, they would have felt lacerated by happiness. Which would have been life. Which would have been beauty.

White pebble

A long time ago she found a white pebble on a beach.
She brushed off the sand and placed it in her pocket,
then put it away in a drawer at home. A pebble worn
smooth and round by the waves' long caress. To her,
its whiteness seemed almost transparent, but when she
tried to peer inside it she found she'd been mistaken.
(In fact, it was a perfectly ordinary white pebble.) Now
and then she got it out and set it on her palm. If silence
could be condensed into the smallest, most solid
object, this is how it would feel, she thought.

White bone

She was once X-rayed to try to determine the cause
of the pain that afflicted her. The skeleton in the
Roentgen ray, gray-white bones in a gunmetal sea. It
startled her to see it like that: something with the solid
materiality of stone, steadfast inside the human body.

A long time before that, around puberty, she
had become fascinated by the names of the various
bones. Anklebone and knee bone. Collarbone and
rib. Breastbone and clavicle, another name for the
collarbone. That human beings are also constructed of
something other than flesh and muscle seemed to her
like a strange stroke of luck.

Sand

And she frequently forgot,
That her body (all our bodies) is a house of sand.
That it had shattered and is shattering still.
Slipping stubbornly through fingers.

White hair

She remembers one of her bosses, a middle-aged man
who used to say how he longed to see a former lover
again in old age, when her hair would be feather-white.
When we're really old . . . when every single strand of our
hair has gone white, I want to see her then, absolutely.

If there was a time when he would want to see her
again, it would certainly be then.

    When both youth and flesh would have fallen away.

    When there would be no time left for desire.

    When only one thing would remain to be done
once that meeting was over: to separate. To part from
their own bodies, and thus to part forever.

Clouds

*That summer, we saw the clouds passing over the fields
while we were sitting out in front of Unju temple, remember?
Huddled together, gazing at the Buddha that had been carved
into the rock's flat surface. Shadows of huge clouds slid
swiftly by, side by side between land and sky.*

Incandescent bulb

Her desk has been swept bare. There is only the incandescent bulb above it, giving off light and heat.

All is still.

The blinds have not been lowered, and headlights can be seen moving along the main road at sporadic intervals now that midnight has passed.

She is sitting at the desk, like someone who has never known suffering.

Not like someone who has just been crying or is about to.

Like someone who has never shattered.

As though there has never been a time when the only comfort lay in the impossibility of forever.

White nights

She learned of its existence after coming to this city: an inhabited island at the northernmost point of Norway, where the summer sun hangs in the sky the whole day, while in winter those twenty-four hours are all night. She wondered what daily life would be like in such an extreme environment. Is the time being measured out around her now another such white night, or is it a black day? Stale pain has not yet withered quite away, fresh pain has not yet burst into bloom. Days in which darkness and light are both imperfect swell with memories of the past. The only things that the mind cannot examine are memories of the future. Ahead of her now is an amorphous light, flickering like some gas of unknown composition.

Island of light

The moment she went up onstage, the ceiling spotlight
flicked on, its strong beam picking her out. At that,
all space that was not the stage became a sea of black.
That an audience was sitting there seemed wholly
unreal and she was thrown into confusion. Do I go
down into that ocean floor, step by faltering step, or
stand my ground here in this island of light?

Black writing through white paper

Each time she groped her way back to health, she would find that life now cast a certain chill. A feeling that it would be too feeble to call "resentment," too severe to call "rancor." As though the one who had been tucking her in and kissing her forehead each night had suddenly turned on her yet again, driving her out of the house into the cold, making her painfully aware that all those sunny smiles had been only on the surface.

Looking at herself in the mirror, she never forgot that death was hovering behind that face. Faint yet tenacious, like black writing bleeding through thin paper.

Learning to love life again is a long and complicated process.

Because at some point you will inevitably cast me aside.

When I am at my weakest, when I am most in
    need of help,
You will turn your back on me, cold and
    irrevocable.
And that is something perfectly clear to me.
And I cannot now return to the time before that
    knowledge.

Scattering

Before the day drew to a close, slushy snow began to fall.

In the blink of an eye, the ash-gray streets of the old town were erased into whiteness. A whiteness that seemed too perfect to be real, showing up the shabby figures that moved against its canvas, their threadbare cloaks of ordinary hours. Like them, she walked without stopping. Through beauty that would disappear—was disappearing already. Mutely.

To the stillness

When the day of her leaving draws near,
and she stands in the darkness of this house,
    there are words she will want to speak to its
    stillness, which she is no longer permitted to
    dwell inside.
When the night that had seemed without end is
    over and the northeastern window is a swatch
    of deep-blue twilight,
when the sky then brightens to ultramarine
    and the clean bones of poplars are slowly
    outlined,
there will be something she wants to say to
    the stillness, in the early hours of Sunday
    morning when the building's other
    inhabitants have yet to stir.

Please, a little longer like this.

To give it time to wash me clean.

Boundary

She grew up inside this story.

She was born prematurely, at seven months. Her
twenty-two-year-old mother was entirely unprepared
when the contractions came. The first frost of the year
was early. Her mother was alone in the house. The
baby cried only briefly after coming into the world,
a thin, wavering sound that soon petered out. Her
mother dressed the small, bloodied body in a baby
gown and wrapped her carefully in a padded quilt,
making sure not to smother her. At first, when the
baby fastened to the empty breast, instinct produced
a feeble sucking, but this, too, soon subsided. The
baby was laid gently down on the warmest part of
the heated floor, but by this point she was no longer
crying, her eyes were no longer open. Now and then
her mother would be struck by a sense of foreboding
and give a corner of the quilt a tug, but the baby's eyes
opened only briefly, grew dim, and then slid shut. At

some point, even that scant response was no longer forthcoming. And yet, before dawn, when the first milk finally came from her mother's breasts and she pressed her nipple between the tiny lips, she found that, despite everything, the baby was still breathing. Though she had, by now, slipped from consciousness, the nipple in her mouth encouraged a soft swallowing, gradually growing stronger. Still with her eyes closed the whole time. Not knowing what boundary she was now passing over.

Reedbed

One morning after a night of snow, she walks into
a reedbed. She parts the reeds, each slender white
stalk bent under the weight of the snow. The reedbed
surrounds a small marsh, where a pair of wild ducks are
living. At its heart, where the thin sheet of ice meets
still water, the ducks float side by side on its grayish-
blue surface, necks bowed to drink.

Before turning back from them, she asks herself: Do
you want to go on? To push forward? Is it worth it?

There was a time when she had answered, trembling, no.
 Now she walks, holding any answer in reserve. She
leaves that semifrozen marsh, between dreariness and
delicacy.

White butterfly

Were it not the case that life stretches out in a straight
line, she might at some point become aware of having
rounded a bend. Bringing, perhaps, the realization that
nothing of that past could now be glimpsed were she to
cast a quick glance over her shoulder. This road might
be covered not with snow or frost but with the soft
tenacity of pale green spring grasses. A white butterfly
stuttering forward might snatch at her gaze, tug her
a few paces farther in the wake of those wingbeats,
like a soul's fretful palpitations. She might become
aware only then of the surrounding trees, their slow
reanimation as though in thrall to something, giving off
a strange and stifling scent, flaring up into a still more
lush proliferation, into thin air, toward the light.

Spirit

Were spirits to exist, she thought, their motion would be the invisible correlate of just such a butterfly's trembling flight.

If that were so, would the souls of this city sometimes drift to the wall where they were once gunned down and flutter there for a time with such a soundless motion? But she knew that the people of this city did not light candles and lay flowers in front of that wall only for the sake of such souls. They believe that there is no shame in having been butchered. They want to draw out their grief for as long as possible.

She thought of certain incidents in her own country's history, the country she had left in order to come here, of the dead that had been insufficiently mourned. Trying to imagine those souls being thus eulogized, in the very heart of the city streets, she realized that her country had never once done this properly.

And, less significantly, she learned what had been

left out of her own reconstruction. Of course, her body had not yet died. Her spirit still had flesh to house it. Like the remaining section of a ruined brick wall, which the bombing had not managed to destroy completely, since moved and incorporated into another structure— from which the blood has been washed clean. Flesh that was now no longer young.

As she walked, she imitated the steady gait of one who had never been broken. A clean cloth veiling each unstitched place. Doing without farewells, without mourning. If she believes that she has never been shattered, she can believe that she will be shattered no more.

And so there are a few things left to her:

To stop lying.

To (open her eyes and) remove the veil.

To light a candle for all the deaths and spirits she can remember—including her own.

Rice raw and cooked

She walks in search of rice to cook for dinner. Finding sticky rice in this city is easier said than done. Even in a large supermarket the closest she gets is some Spanish rice, sold in small plastic packs of five hundred grams. The white grains lie quiet in her bag as she carries them home. White steam rises from the bowl of just-cooked rice, and she sits in front of it as though at prayer. She cannot deny that, at that moment, she feels something inside her. To deny it is impossible.

3

———

ALL WHITENESS

모

든

흰

The year after she lost her first child, she had another premature birth. I was told that the baby, a boy this time, managed even fewer months in the womb than the girl had, and died soon after being born, without once opening his eyes. Had those lives made it safely past the point of crisis, my own birth, which followed three years later, and that of my brother four years after that, would not have come about. My mother would not have lived with those shattered memories inside her, running her fingers carefully over their sharp edges.

This life needed only one of us to live it. If you had lived beyond those first few hours, I would not be living now.

My life means yours is impossible.

Only in the gap between darkness and light, only in that blue-tinged breach, do we manage to make out each other's faces.

Your eyes

I saw differently when I looked with your eyes. I
walked differently when I walked with your body. I
wanted to show you clean things. Before brutality,
sadness, despair, filth, pain, clean things that were only
for you, clean things above all. But it didn't come off as
I intended. Again and again I peered into your eyes, as
though searching for form in a deep, black mirror.

If only we'd been living in a city back then, I heard my
mother say several times during my childhood. If only
an ambulance could have taken me to the hospital. If
only they'd put her in an incubator, that tiny rice cake
of a baby. They were a new thing then, incubators.

If only you hadn't stopped breathing. And had
therefore been granted all this life in my stead, I
who would then never have been born. If it had been
granted to you to go firmly forward, with your own
eyes and your own body, your back to that dark mirror.

Shroud

What did you do with her, with the baby?

The night I first asked my father this, when I was almost out of my teens and he was not yet fifty, he was silent for a while before answering.

Wrapped her in a white shroud, took her to the mountain, and buried her.

Alone?

That's right. Alone.

The girl's baby gown became a shroud. Her swaddling bands became a coffin.

After he went to bed, I stopped on my way to get a drink of water and straightened my stiff, hunched shoulders. With my hand pressed to my breastbone, I drew a breath in.

Onni

I used to think of what it would be like if I'd had an older sister. An onni a hand's span taller than me. An onni to hand down slightly bobbled sweaters, patent leather shoes with only minor scuff marks.

An onni who would shrug on her coat and go to the pharmacy when our mother was ill. An onni who would put her finger to her lips and scold me: *Quietly, you have to walk quietly.* An onni who could write out equations in my math workbook. *This is really simple, you're just overthinking it.* Frowning as she hurried to reach the solution.

An onni who would tell me to sit down when I got a splinter in my foot. Who would bring the lamp over and, in its light, extract the splinter, ever so carefully, with a needle that she'd sterilized in the flame from the gas range.

An onni to come over when I'm huddled in the dark. *There's no need for that, it's all a misunderstanding.* A brief, awkward embrace. *Get up, for goodness' sake. Now let's eat.* A cold hand grazing my face. Her shoulders slipping swiftly away.

Like a clutch of words strewn over white paper

My black shoes stamped prints into the early-morning snow, a slushy layer sheeting the pavement.

Like a clutch of words strewn over white paper.

Seoul, which I had last seen in summer, had frozen.

Turning to look behind me, I saw the snow already sifting down to cover those just-made prints.

Whitening.

Mourning robes

Before two people get married, each gives clothes to
the other's parents. Silk clothes for those still living,
cotton mourning robes for the departed.

My brother called to check that I would go with
him. *I waited until you came back, nuna.*

The woman he was to marry had prepared a white
cotton skirt and jacket, which I spread out on the rock.
In a meadow of long grasses beneath the temple where
our mother's name is chanted after each morning's
sutras. As soon as I held my brother's lighter to the
sleeve, a thread of blue-tinged smoke spiraled up. After
white clothes dissolve into the air this way, a spirit will
wear them. Do we really believe that?

Smoke

We kept our eyes fixed intently on what was in front of
us, our mouths tightly shut. Smoke like a pair of ash-
gray wings was dissolving into the air. Disappearing. I
saw the fire, having consumed the jacket, run instantly
onto the skirt. When the last strip of cloth was
swallowed by the flames, I thought of you. If you can
come to us now, then do. Slip on those clothes that the
fire has borne to you, like slipping on a pair of wings.
Drink it like medicine or tea, our silence, dissolving
into smoke in place of words.

Silence

When long days finally come to a close, a time to be
quiet is needed. As when, unconsciously in front of a
stove, I hold my stiff hands out to the silence, fingers
splayed in its scant warmth.

Lower teeth

The pronunciation of "onni" resembles that of a baby's "lower teeth." Two tiny teeth like first leaves that had sprouted from my son's gums.

Now my son has grown up and is no longer a baby. After pulling the quilt up to cover that twelve-year-old boy, I listened carefully for a while to his steady breathing before returning to my empty desk.

Parting

Don't die. For God's sake don't die.

I open my lips and mutter the words you heard on opening your black eyes, you who were ignorant of language. I press down with all my strength onto the white paper. I believe that no better words of parting can be found. *Don't die. Live.*

All whiteness

With your eyes, I will see the deepest, most dazzling place within a white cabbage, the precious young petals concealed at its heart.

With your eyes, I will see the chill of the half-moon risen in the day.

At some point those eyes will see a glacier. They will look up at that enormous mass of ice and see something sacred, unsullied by life.

They will see inside the silence of the white birch forest. Inside the stillness of the window where the winter sun seeps in. Inside those shining grains of dust, swaying along the shafts of light that slant onto the ceiling.

Within that white, all of those white things, I will breathe in the final breath you released.

About the Author

HAN KANG was born in 1970 in South Korea. She is the author of *The Vegetarian*, winner of the International Booker Prize, as well as *Human Acts*, *The White Book*, *Greek Lessons*, and *We Do Not Part*. In 2024, she was awarded the Nobel Prize in Literature.

DEBORAH SMITH has translated books by Han Kang and Bae Suah. She founded Tilted Axis Press in 2015 and is based in north India.

han-kang.net